Sea ost

story by Priscilla Galloway • pictures by Karen Patkau

Annick Press
Toronto

© 1988 Priscilla Galloway (text)
© 1988 Karen Patkau (art)

Annick Press gratefully acknowledges
the contributions of the Canada Council
and the Ontario Arts Council

Design by Karen Patkau

Photography by See Spot Run

Canadian Cataloguing in Publication Data

Galloway, Priscilla, 1930–
Seal is lost

ISBN 1-55037-019-7 (bound) ISBN 1-55037-018-9 (pbk.)

I. Patkau, Karen. II. Title.

PS8563.A44S42 1988   jC813′.54   C88-094080-8
PZ7.G34Se 1988

Distributed in Canada and the USA by:
Firefly Books Ltd.
3520 Pharmacy Avenue, Unit 1-C
Scarborough, Ontario
M1W 2T8

Printed and bound in Canada by
D.W. Friesen & Sons

for my grandsons Ryan and Hugh

Seal always cuddles under Hugh's left arm. When Hugh wants to play in the sandbox, Seal wants to play in the sandbox. When Hugh goes to sleep, Seal goes too.

But suddenly Hugh misses Seal. There's a big empty space under his arm where Seal should be. Seal is not there. Seal is lost. "I'll help you look," says Dad. "Seal can't be far away."

But Seal is far away. Seal is in Lost Toyland. She has a bright red lost bicycle to ride, and a big red lost ball to balance on her nose. The lost teddies and dolls shout, "Hurray for Seal."

Seal likes the other lost toys. She likes riding the lost bicycle. But she misses Hugh. Her flippers feel all tingly when she thinks about him.

"I hear Seal calling me," says Hugh. "Is Seal behind the couch?" Mum and Hugh pull the couch out. They find two books, three blocks, five crayons and one dusty quarter, but no Seal. "Where are you, Seal?" calls Hugh.

Seal knows Hugh is calling because her flippers feel all tingly. But Seal does not want to go home. She has found a very long skipping rope, and some of her new friends are very good at turning double dutch.

"Seal is scratching at the front door," says Hugh. "She wants to come in."

Mum unlocks the door.

No Seal.

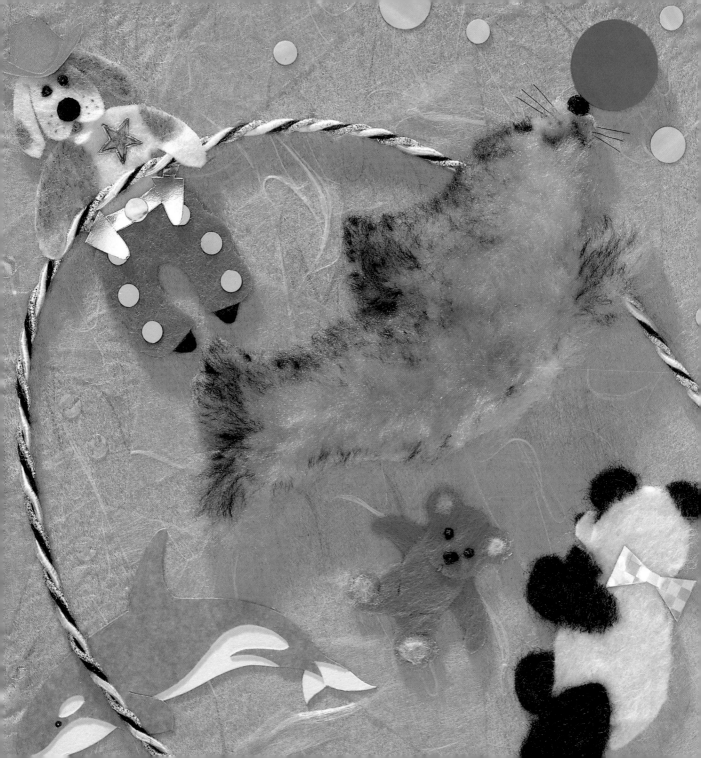

On the doorstep, there is a very wet, very muddy, little kitten. Hugh picks up the kitten.

"We have to find out who she belongs to," Mum says.

"I like this kitten," says Hugh. "I'm going to call her Ginger. But Seal is still calling to me," he says. "Maybe Seal is in my bed."

Seal still does not want to come home from Lost Toyland. She wants Hugh to be a pirate too.

In the kitchen of the lost dolls' house, Seal and her friends make pizza with all the trimmings, especially anchovies. Seal loves anchovies. Hugh hates them. Seal makes part of the pizza without any anchovies, just for Hugh. But Hugh is not in Lost Toyland.

Back at home, Hugh's Mum says, "We have to make a notice. Then whoever lost Ginger can get her back."

"Maybe they don't want her back," says Hugh. "Let's make a notice about Seal too," he says. "You can help."

One family phones about Ginger. "Does she have blue eyes?" they ask. Ginger has green eyes.

One family comes to see Ginger. "Our kitten was bigger," they say.

The other people are sad because they have not found their kitten. Hugh is happy. "Now we have to keep Ginger," he says.

Not even one person phones about Seal.

Why should anybody phone about Seal? Hugh can't find her, but she is safe in Lost Toyland. She is playing house with her friends.

"I'll be the Daddy," Seal says.

Nobody says, "You can't be the Daddy because you're a girl."

Hugh used to love taking Seal to school. "You can't take Ginger," says Mum. "You can't take a pet to school."

"Some days we have pet days," says Hugh. But they don't have pet days very often. "I really miss Seal," says Hugh.

Hugh loves Ginger, but he is lonely for Seal. Supergran comes to visit. "Write a letter to Seal," she says. "I can send it to her with my magic wand."

Hugh writes a letter and reads it to Supergran. "Can Seal read my letter?" he asks.

"My magic wand will help," says Supergran. She mutters a word or two, and Hugh's letter disappears.

"Seal has got your letter," says Supergran. "I can see her jumping up and down on her flippers. She is very happy. She loves you too."

"I want to see Seal," says Hugh.

"You have your own magic," replies Supergran. "Everybody has their own magic. Close your eyes. Now think about Seal and make a wish-picture in your head. Make a wish-picture so you can see Lost Toyland. Seal is in Lost Toyland with all the other lost toys. Can you see her there?"

"No," says Hugh.

"Try again," says Supergran.

Hugh closes his eyes very tight. "I can see her," he shouts. "I can really see Seal."

Suddenly there is a meow. Ginger has climbed up the drapes and is hanging there.

"Ginger was lonely," says Hugh. "I'll get you down, Ginger."

"You're my cat now," says Hugh.